THE BELL WITCH

GHOST OF TENNESSEE

Retold by
MATT BOUGIE

Illustrated by
BRIAN GARVEY

Cavendish
Square

New York

NOT LONG AFTER THE REVOLUTIONARY WAR, Americans sought new lands to farm and explore. In 1796, Tennessee joined the United States, and many Americans on the East Coast moved there to claim land. One of those people was Mr. John Bell.

Mr. Bell bought a house and some farmland near the Red River. He planted crops and harvested them. He was a successful farmer and bought more and more land. Everything seemed to be going well for him and his family.

One day, after fifteen years of successful planting and harvesting, Mr. Bell was walking through the corn rows to see if they were ready to harvest. Suddenly, he spied something small and furry between the leaves. *That must be a rabbit trying to steal my corn!* Mr. Bell thought as he readied his rifle.

Mr. Bell peered through the stalks of corn, stepping carefully so as not to trample his crops. After a few moments, he stood in the same row as the animal. It looked much bigger than the rabbits Mr. Bell was used to—more like a dog or a coyote. The strange creature didn't move or react as Mr. Bell approached. It only stared at him.

Mr. Bell raised his gun and breathed as he pulled the trigger. The shot missed, and the animal finally moved. But it didn't run like a dog. It sprang like a rabbit, quickly darting out of sight. Mr. Bell was unnerved, but he continued inspecting the corn for harvest.

After a few days, Mr. Bell forgot about the strange creature and the way it stared at him. He forgot about it until one night when he was woken from a deep sleep. A scraping sound was coming from upstairs. He sat up in bed and lit a candle. *The children must have let a stray dog in the house*, he thought. *I told them not to bring animals into the house.*

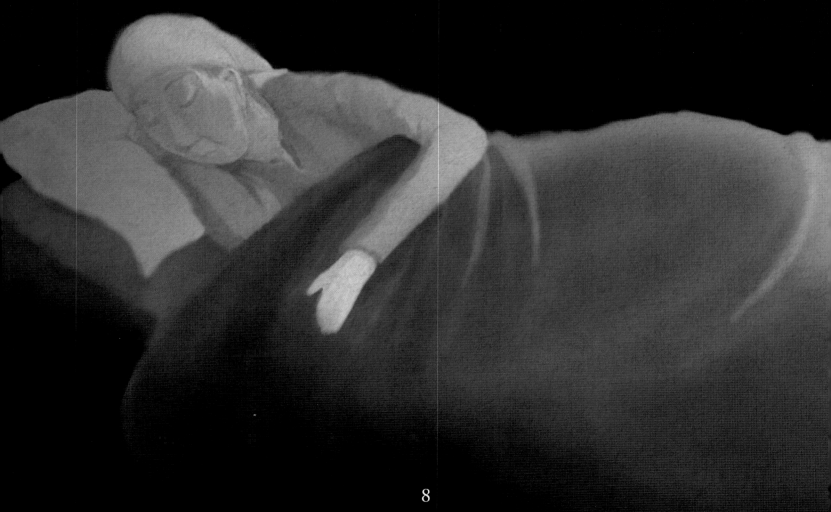

As he walked up the stairs, the scratching noise got louder and faster. Mr. Bell also began to hear a whisper. With each step he took, the whispering got louder and more frantic, until all he heard was quiet laughter.

Mr. Bell's hand reached for the doorknob and he began to twist and push, but the door seemed stuck. The laughing grew louder and rang in Mr. Bell's ears. He put his shoulder against the door and forced it open. But the room was empty and the laughing had stopped. For the first time in a long time, Mr. Bell was afraid. He slowly walked back downstairs, listening for claws scraping against the floor, but everything was silent.

The next morning at breakfast, Mr. Bell asked his children about the noises. Betsy Bell, John Bell's daughter, told her father that she had also heard the noises but was too afraid to leave her bed. "There was a voice in the dark last night. She was laughing at me and throwing my books across the room. I couldn't see her, but I knew she was there. It felt like she was poking me with pins!"

As Betsy was talking, all the breakfast dishes were pushed off the table and tumbled to the floor with a clang. The entire Bell family looked at each other with fear.

Mr. Bell spoke. "Hello? Who's there? Who is this? Why are you here?" There was no one there, but a voice whispered, "Kate," and nothing else.

After that morning, "Kate" was a regular visitor at the Bell farm. Some nights she was content to drag ropes and chains across the upstairs hallways and move tables and chairs into doorways. When Mr. Bell would trip over a newly moved chair, the entire house would rattle with Kate's cackle.

Some nights were much worse. Kate would visit the children and pinch and poke them. They would wake up with bruises and cuts across their arms, legs, and faces.

Sometimes she would call them names or follow them as they went out into the woods to play. Betsy was Kate's favorite target.

Betsy Bell started noticing a young man named Joshua Gardner. Joshua lived near the Bell farm, and the two grew up playing together. One day, the two decided that they wanted to marry each other. The entire family was happy for the young couple. Everyone thought it was a good match, and they eagerly looked forward to the wedding. Everyone except Kate.

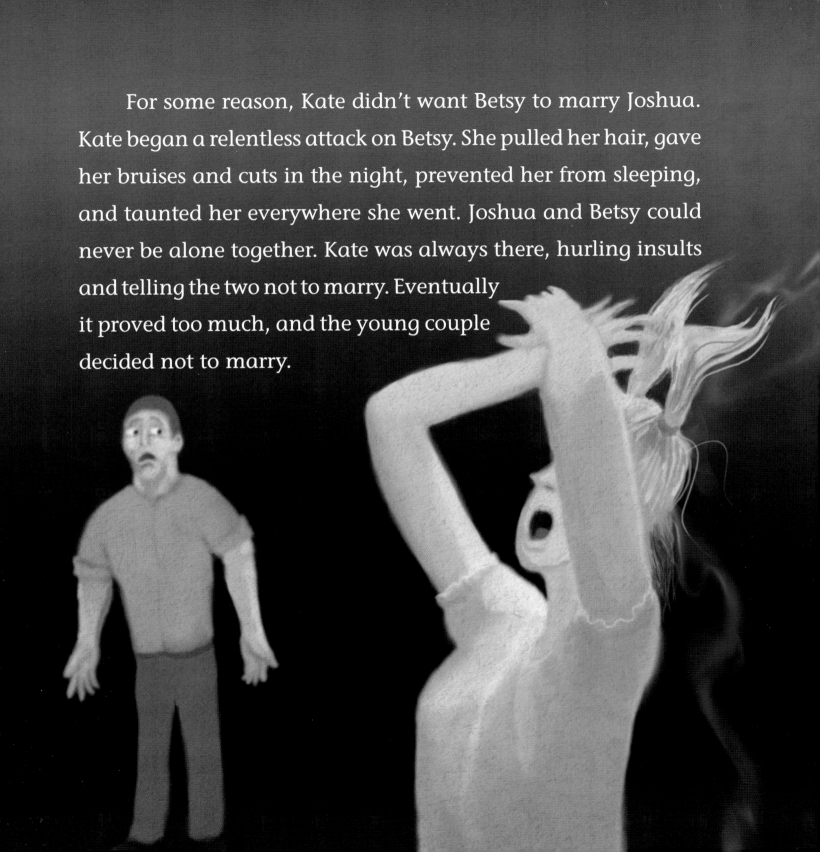

For some reason, Kate didn't want Betsy to marry Joshua. Kate began a relentless attack on Betsy. She pulled her hair, gave her bruises and cuts in the night, prevented her from sleeping, and taunted her everywhere she went. Joshua and Betsy could never be alone together. Kate was always there, hurling insults and telling the two not to marry. Eventually it proved too much, and the young couple decided not to marry.

If Betsy was Kate's favorite target, Mr. Bell was the person that Kate hated above anyone else. When Mr. Bell asked his neighbors to come over and help him drive out the witch, Kate would mock Mr. Bell and tell rumors and secrets about his guests. None of Mr. Bell's many friends could figure out how to calm Kate down or how to keep her from tormenting Mr. Bell.

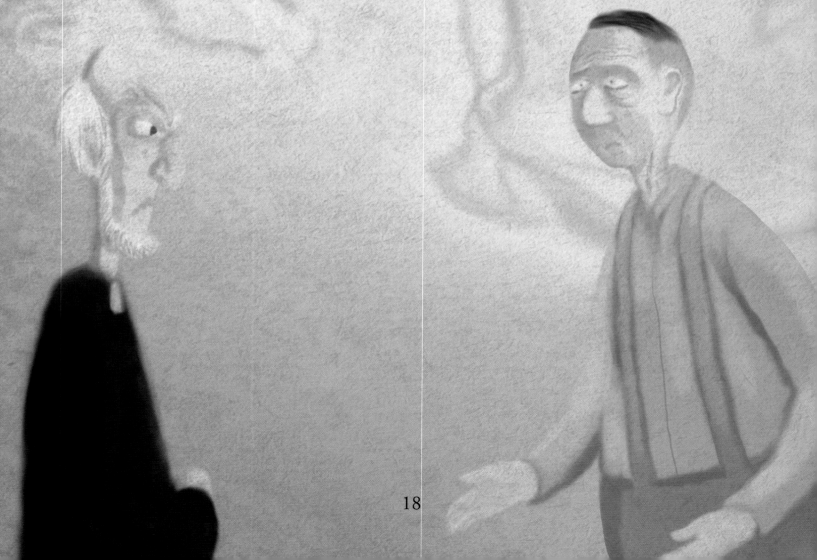

It seemed that Kate's mission was to drive him to his deathbed. In the months and years after Mr. Bell shot at the strange animal in his cornfield, his health grew worse and worse. He began having frequent convulsions that left him so weak that he could not leave his bed for days at a time.

One morning when Mr. Bell was feeling better than usual, he laced up his shoes and headed outside to feed the pigs. As he was walking, he noticed that his shoes came untied—so he stopped and stooped over to retie them. He took one more step and both his shoelaces were untied again. *How peculiar,* he thought.

John Bell bent down to tie his shoes again, making sure that they were as tight as he could make them. He felt something push him from behind. He fell flat on his stomach. His shoes flew off his feet and landed in the grass. He gathered them, slid them back on his feet, and laced them with strong double knots. While it was strange, Mr. Bell was accustomed to Kate's tricks.

After the pigs were fed and happy, Mr. Bell began walking back toward the house. He never used to get so tired so easily, but ever since Kate showed up, he'd been tired and frail. Halfway up the path, Mr. Bell felt something grab his ankle. He fell again, and his shoes were torn from his feet. Kate laughed and laughed as he struggled to stand. After several minutes, Mrs. Bell looked out the window and saw John trying to gather his shoes from the grass.

Mrs. Bell helped John back into the house and laid him down in bed. Mr. Bell's face was pale and his eyes looked empty. Battling with Kate day and night for all those years had taken its toll on him. He grew very ill and could not leave his bed. All the while, Kate laughed and laughed at poor Mr. Bell.

That winter was not a good one for the Bell family. Mr. Bell became very ill one morning and fell into a coma. The next day, he passed away without speaking or waking again.

ABOUT THE BELL WITCH

The Bell Witch is a legend about the haunting of a farm in northern Tennessee. It is said that the Bell Witch first appeared in 1817 and that most of the strange activity ended in 1821. While no one is sure of what actually happened during those years, the Bell Witch legend is still important to the people who live near the old farm.

While John Bell was the only confirmed "casualty" of the haunting, the witch terrorized most members of the family to one degree or another. Many neighbors reported hearing a strange voice while visiting the farm—a voice that knew deep, dark secrets they had never told anyone before.

Some say that the Bell Witch was actually a neighbor of John Bell named Kate Batts. Some people think Kate Batts was an actual witch or ghost. Others claim that she was simply someone to blame for something unexplained. The mystery continues to this day.

WORDS TO KNOW

cackle A noisy and unpleasant laugh.

convulsions Sudden, violent, or irregular movements of a limb or of the body.

frail Very weak.

relentless Continuing without any relief.

unnerved Afraid or upset.

TO FIND OUT MORE

BOOKS

Fitzhugh, Pat. *The Bell Witch: The Full Account.* Ashland City, TN: The Armand Press. 2000.

Ingram, M.V. *An Authenticated History of the Famous Bell Witch.* 1894.

WEBSITES

The Bell Witch Hauntings

http://archive.org/stream/TheBellWitchPdf/TheBellWitch_djvu.txt

This is the earliest account of the Bell Witch haunting. Many people are interviewed and give their own accounts of what happened on the Bell farm.

The Bell Witch Website

http://www.bellwitch.org

This site gives a nice retelling of the story of the Bell Witch. It offers a timeline, a list of prominent figures in the legend, and an FAQ.

ABOUT THE AUTHOR

Matt Bougie grew up in a small town in central Wisconsin. After graduating from St. Norbert College, he moved to Milwaukee, Wisconsin, to pursue a career. He continues to live there, working at a marketing company and as a freelance writer. In his free time, he enjoys watching sports, riding his bicycle, or playing with his dogs.

ABOUT THE ILLUSTRATOR

Brian Garvey has been drawing since he was a young kid growing up in Ohio. His fascination with the creative arts led him to study illustration at Rhode Island School of Design, graduating with a BFA and eventually moving to Brooklyn, New York, where he currently resides. When not working or sleeping, he enjoys watching movies, running, and doing yoga. He is currently working on his own graphic novel, and more examples of his work can be found at http://www.sengarden.com.

Published in 2017 by Cavendish Square Publishing, LLC
243 5th Avenue, Suite 136, New York, NY 10016

Cataloging-in-Publication Data

Names: Bougie, Matt.
Title: The Bell Witch: ghost of Tennessee / Matt Bougie.
Description: New York : Cavendish Square Publishing, 2017. |
Series: American legends and folktales | Includes index.
Identifiers: ISBN 9781502622204 (pbk.) | ISBN 9781502622235 (library bound) |
ISBN 9781502622228 (6 pack) | ISBN 9781502622242 (ebook)
Subjects: LCSH: Bell family--Fiction. | Poltergeists--Tennessee--Fiction.
Classification: LCC PZ7.B635 Be 2017 | DDC [F]--dc23

Editorial Director: David McNamara
Editor: Kristen Susienka
Copy Editor: Nathan Heidelberger
Associate Art Director: Amy Greenan
Designer: Alan Sliwinski
Illustrator: Brian Garvey
Production Coordinator: Karol Szymczuk

Printed in the United States of America